U Did It Gurl
Empowerment Journal

Sophia Yamia Degraffenreid

ACKNOWLEDGMENTS

I want to first acknowledge my Father God, (Jehovah) God, for His grace and mercy over my mind and life. I thank him for allowing me to have my sanity after so many advertisers in my life. I thank him for allowing me to share my testimony with the world. I thank you, Father God, in Jesus Christ my Lord and Savior mighty name.

Much love and appreciation to my Bae, Mr. Leander W. Patton, my love for staying by my side and loving me unconditionally, even when we both could not understand what I was dealing with. I thank you, Wayne, for your calm, humbling, cool spirit when mine was raging. Thank you, Bae, for always reminding me to relax, calm down, lay down, and his favorite line, "Eat your food Sophie" when I didn't know when to shut down.

I love and appreciate you, Wayne, for stepping in and taking on Kenneth Jr. and my princess Donnae; as your own children. You gave them a Father's experience that I could not. Thank you, Bae, for giving me the most beautiful baby girls, now teens, a mommy can ask for. Our ladybug Dejah and Princess Destiny. I love you, Bae, and I am grateful to God to have you as my love.

To the best, most intelligent son a mother could ask for, my amazing son, Kenneth D. Grays Jr., whom I love and admire so much. He will always have his mommy's back, no matter what! I thank you, son, for being my "ride to live." Thank you, son, for being by my side through my difficulties and never giving up on me during my Mental illnesses.

Thank you, son, for every phone call and text message you sent me to make sure I was ok. I thank you for always trying to feed your mommy and making sure your sisters, and I were all good. Mommy loves you, son, more than words can say.

I give God all the glory for giving me such an angel like you. May you follow the plans God has for you and allow your goals, dreams, and visions to birth and make room for you. Thank you, Kenneth, for giving your Mommy hope and A REASON TO FIGHT THIS THING CALLED MENTAL ILLNESS. I LOVE YOU, SON.

Thank you, son, for every phone call and text message you sent me to make sure I was ok. I thank you for always trying to feed your mommy and making sure your sisters, and I were all good. Mommy loves you, son, more than words can say. I give God all the glory for giving me such an angel like you. May you follow the plans God has for you and allow your goals, dreams, and visions to birth and make room for you. Thank you, Kenneth, for giving your Mommy hope and A REASON TO FIGHT THIS THING CALLED MENTAL ILLNESS. I LOVE YOU, SON.

To such a talented, beautiful Queen, and amazing mother, my oldest daughter, my Princess. No matter how old she gets, she is my business manager. When I allow my emotions to take over instead of my business mind, my Donnae, always reminds me, "Ma, do you want to make some money? Or help everyone and be broke?" She does not say much, but it is something to listen to, and she can inspire you when she does.

Princess Donnae, Mommy loves you so much, and I am so thankful you are my miracle! I appreciate and thank God for listening to me on my good days and my bad days. On days I called crying so upset when things overwhelmed Me. I am so blessed and grateful for you listening to me and responding so calmly. You ALWAY keep it real and manage to stay humble. I so appreciate you being here for your sisters and me. You play such an important role in all our lives. You are our influencer! Thank you for being "The Young Lady" who can inspire your mommy and sisters. You, Donnae K. Stamps, are a true example of ~U Did It Gurl, Empowerment, Incorporated~.

You are one of my four reasons I had to fight against this thing called mental illness. You are one of my four reasons U Did It Gurl Empowerment needed to be birthed.

Thank you, Princess, for GIVING ME A REASON!! A VISION! A PURPOSE TO BIRTH THIS THING CALLED #UDIDITGURL and keep my hope alive.

I love you, Donnae, and I know you will be a successful Billionaire! Just keep Mommy on V.I.P., keep making my wigs, and keep slaying my make-up, so I can stay looking fabulous and feeling good inside and out. Thank you, Donnae, for supporting me in all I do. U DID IT GURL, and Mommy LOVES YOU TO LIFE.

Dejah... I thank God every day for you! Mommy loves you so much!! I'm proud of you! Know That! #UDIDITGURLS!

A Dedication To My Mother

I dedicate this book journal to my beautiful mother, Sarai E. Fox, the "QUEEN" of U DID IT GURL Empowerment, Incorporated. The "Seasoned Woman" who has truly inspired me to be all of who I am today. I have watched my mother suffer from mental illness since I can remember, all the way to mental health recovery.

My mother has experienced traumas in her life, and for whatever reason, my mommy was one who battled some serious mental illness, but I will allow the Queen to share her story.

I just want to thank my mother for never giving up and never leaving her family in the midst of her Mental Illness chapters. I want my mother, Sarai E. Fox to know, I so LOVE YOU MOMMY, and I am truly grateful and blessed to have you as my mother. I am thankful to GOD for answering my prayers and healing your mind of Mental illness and allowing you to be HAPPY AND FREE from bondage! I am extremely grateful for my mommy! I LOVE YOU 'GURL!'.

My mommy is such a beautiful, humble, sharp little woman, and because of her sewing into my life at such an early age (From every talent show on the north side of Chicago to the west side of Chicago) and singing in church choirs. To dance classes & church choirs in Kenosha, WI, to singing in the church choir in Zion, Illinois. I was able to sew these same things into for my four children's lives.

My mother made sure she left that legacy with my four sisters and I. Thank You for working so hard to make sure your four daughters were successful. I am so grateful to our Heavenly Father God that my mommy, just celebrated her 60th birthday, November 25, 2020, and is recovering very well from her mental illnesses. She is getting her mental health back and living her best life. I Love You, Mommy. I am so proud of you and your accomplishments in recovery.

WHAT A MIGHTY GOD WE SERVE. I KNEW HE WOULD HEAL YOU! U did it, gurl, and you are rocking your world.

Contents

A Special Thank You To My Grandmother

A special thank you, and I LOVE You, to my beautiful, praying, loving, caring, *DROP IT LIKE IT'S HOT* dancing grandmother Ms. Roberta L. Butler, who has always taken all her children and grandchildren in no matter when or where. To a humbled loving grandmother, "Bigma," who still makes time at age 88 to call and check on my four children and I to make sure we are always ok. I appreciate my grandmother's beautiful cards and the dollars she adds to those cards throughout the year.

I so love you, Bigma, for allowing me to work with you in your beautiful daycare center, Smiling Faces Daycare, Grayslake, Illinois, and allowing me to be your assistant as you traveled as a Child Development Educator. I was so inspired by your educational teachings and was reminded to stay home and raise my children instead of leaving and working outside the home. Thank you, Bigma, for being the SEASONED WOMAN who has inspired my children and I. LOVE YOU, BIGMA!! Thank You for ALWAYS SUPPORTING ME!!

To a very special sister (born my cousin), Crystal Dupree, I want to thank you so much, Vita' Gurl, for being my coach and influencer. Thank you, sis, for the many phone calls and for supporting me from the first day I shared my goals, dreams, and visions.

(And might I add a whole lot of other stuff!! LOL) Thank you, sis, for the best Thanksgiving a gurl could ask for! That Dressing and Homemade mac' and cheese, though! Thank you for always saying, "Just do it, gurl, Sophia!" And you were so serious.

Thank You for starting the hashtag on Instagram #UDIDITGURL for my song "You Did It Gurl,

Anthem," which has now grown into the U Did It Gurl Empowerment Inc and Journal Book.

Thank you, love, for introducing me to Credit Karma four years ago, where I learned how to pick up the pieces to my credit and value my credit so I can own property like You. Thank YOU, MY BEAUTIFUL SISTER, Crystal Dupree, for paving the way for our family by being an example of a true successful ~U Did It Gurl Empowerment Influencer.

I love You, and I am truly thankful to GOD to have you as my cousin and SISTER!!

I know your beautiful mommy, my auntie Roberta "Nancy" Hudson (Rest in Paradise Auntie), would be so PROUD OF HER BABY GURL! I LOVE YOU, AUNTIE NANCY. THANK YOU FOR BLESSING US WITH SUCH AN ANGEL.

To my dearest Auntie, Ms. Patricia Hudson, the lady who has answered all my calls for over twenty-four years, when my mommy could not due to her mental health issues. The auntie who was able to identify my mental health was failing me! The women who told me, back in 2007, "Sophie, do you need an antidepressant?" When I had no knowledge of an antidepressant. The lady who saved my sanity. The auntie who is to be honored for bringing mental illness awareness to me.

A special thank you to Auntie Patty for building extra ears to listen to me through the years. Thank you for all the calls checking on me, my four children, and my mommy. Thank you, auntie, for all the laughs in the midst of my tears when talking to you. Thank you, auntie, for every card of encouragement you mailed me through the years. Thank you for still finding time today to call and text me during such a time for you and being able to check on me and make me laugh! Thank you for all the watchtowers to help give me hope and encouragement. Thank you for being that "Seasoned Woman" of U Did It Gurl, Empowerment, incorporated who can inspire.

I Love you, Auntie Patty. I so appreciate all you have done for me, my children, and my mother. Thank you so much for supporting all my goals, dreams, and visions.

I want to say thank you to all my family and friends who have ever listened to me, prayed for me, and my mental health recovery.

Thank you to everyone who decided to pick up this journal and experience my world for a moment; while identifying and attending to your mental health and awakening your goals, visions, and dreams.

To my big cousin, Big RIDE, (Mr. James Potts voice) "If you smell something stinking, it might just be me, because I'm the dang ole Sh*t!"

May you rest in heaven, cousin James, and sing with the angels. I am going to wear that saying out every time I need to remind myself of who I am, as you left this legacy with us. I love you, James Potts. You are deeply missed. YOU WILL NEVER BE FORGOTTEN.

Thank you for supporting my four children and me. You always visited us and lightened up everybody's heart. Thank you for listening to me cry and never judging me when I was not myself. I know you would be proud of me and say, "Sophie stop the shenanigans, you good! It's Cool Babee!"

In Loving Memory of my cousin, James Potts.

Notes

Notes

Notes

Notes

Affirmation Of The Day

~I Am A Successful Woman, Mom, Daughter, Sister, and Friend. I will LOVE MYSELF from within~.

~Do not look at your "right now" and feel as though this is the end. It is the beginning, my sister!! YES, YOU WILL WIN~

~ I am beautiful, inside and out, and I will walk with confidence, love, and joy! No more doubt~

~I am BEAUTIFUL!

I AM FREE!

I WILL LOVE MYSELF EVERY DAY, AND

I WILL WALK IN MY God-Given DESTINY! ~

~Do not claim or speak negativity over your life because you are a STRONG, BEAUTIFUL WOMAN THAT GOD CREATED TO PRODUCE MORE LIFE! ~

Notes

Notes

Notes

Notes

Free My Mind, Spoken Word

If my mind is not free, I cannot walk in my God-given destiny.

If I cannot free my mind, I cannot walk into God's plan, Divine.

If my mind is not free, I cannot function- My gums, my teeth, it's time to clean, or there will be bacteria or an infection.

If my mind is not free, I tend to worry, and my mind is blocked. It fails to tell the cells in my body to cleanse the arteries. (Stroke)

If my mind is not free, it cannot speak to my body's organs and cells. A person can be stress-free and not experience the enemy cancer; Cancer that can grow inside of thee.

If my mind is not free, it cannot function to my intestines, so I can release the toxins that don't belong inside of my body

If my mind is not free, it can't tell the heart to LOVE one another, as it says in second 2nd Corinthians....

If my mind is not free, I cannot love on my children, care for them, and be the mother GOD created me to be for my precious babies.

If my mind is not free, I cannot see clearly and walk on the path God has set forth for me.

If my mind is not free, I can't speak from the heart rationally.

Now you tell me, what does it mean to you when you say if my mind is not free?

Notes

_____
_____
_____
_____
_____
_____
_____
_____
_____
_____
_____
_____
_____
_____
_____
_____
_____
_____
_____
_____
_____
_____
_____
_____
_____
_____
_____
_____
_____
_____
_____

Notes

TOPIC: _____

Notes

TOPIC:_____

Notes

Jeremiah 29:11

For I know the thoughts that I think toward you, saith the Lord, thoughts of peace, and not of evil, to give you an expected end.

DESTINY

My Destiny is greater than my pain, came to me as your first name.

During the time I conceived you, I thought my love was being true, only to find out he rejected not just you, but me too.

Thanks to my Father God, I made it through.

So many times, we cannot understand where all the underline, hurt, anger, and frustration began. But baby girl, I am here to tell you, it started deep within.

Now that we made it through those emotional nine months, Lord knows I was so happy when I was finally able to hold and touch my precious Buttercup.

Just as healthy as you can be, girl, when you came out, you were mommies DESTINY!

Notes

Notes

_____
_____
_____
_____
_____
_____
_____
_____
_____
_____
_____
_____
_____
_____
_____
_____
_____
_____
_____
_____
_____
_____
_____
_____
_____
_____
_____
_____
_____
_____
_____
_____
_____
_____
_____
_____
_____

Notes

Notes

Psalm 46:5

*God is in the midst of her; she
shall not be moved: God shall help
her, and that right early.*

No Validation Needed

You see, you cannot possibly understand my purpose, my calling, or my destiny because those seeds were planted by God, just for me.

No need to try and get validation ANYMORE from anyone. God is the only validation and confirmation I need.

Continuing my journey strong and confident, I hope you are too. It's time I (WE) Release that spirit of fear, validations of others, and accept the confirmations from God! Walk-in your purpose, calling, and Destiny, because thank God, I am now free

Notes

Notes

_____
_____
_____
_____
_____
_____
_____
_____
_____
_____
_____
_____
_____
_____
_____
_____
_____
_____
_____
_____
_____
_____
_____
_____
_____
_____
_____
_____
_____
_____
_____

Notes

Notes

TOPIC:_____

Romans 8:31

What shall we then say to these things? If God be for us, who can be against us?

Inspirational Read

It was when my mindset changed; I realized I needed a new game. To get us poverty-free and get past my pain.

I did not do it to put on a show; I did it because this is what I know to be the best way to go.

After my dreams, visions, and goals, yes, this is how I flow.

For my children and I, and the only way to open this legacy door.

DO NOT STOP BELIEVING, AND ACHIEVING, KEEP PUSHING UNTIL IT BECOMES YOUR REALITY...

#BELIEVING #MOVINGFORWARD #REALITY
#PROUDBLACKWOMEN
#BLACKOWNEDNUSINESS
#PROVERTYFREE   #EPIC   #REHOBOTH
#SUITE10

Notes

_____
_____
_____
_____
_____
_____
_____
_____
_____
_____
_____
_____
_____
_____
_____
_____
_____
_____
_____
_____
_____
_____
_____
_____
_____
_____
_____
_____
_____
_____
_____

Notes

Notes

TOPIC: _____

Notes

Philippians 4:13

I can do all things through Christ which strengtheneth me.

Inspirational Read

When the world is shaken; and You have no clue what to do

during the COVID-19 PANDEMIC...

Do not lose Faith, Hope, or get the blues. Put on the whole armor of God and keep walking in Faith so God can use you.

The girls and I will be home-schooled and study.

Learning the word of God, training them on how to pray, and teaching Spanish.

#havefaith #holdongodisnotdonewithus #prayersup #thewholearmourofgodofgod #blessings

#udiditgurl

Notes

TOPIC: _____

Notes

Notes

Notes

Ephesians 6:11

*Put on the whole armour of God,
that ye may be able to stand
against the wiles of the devil.*

FREE MY MIND WIG LINE

Free my mind is a wig line I created while suffering from mental illnesses in 2019.

After treatment, I learned of something called mindfulness, and in mindfulness, I decided I would use my skills of hair care by creating custom wigs, and crochet braiding to help me stand in place of mindfulness.

I was temporarily disabled due to mental illness and found myself bored during that time. Being idle, I learned a thing or two about finding a happy place. My happy place is doing hair. My hair care line is Free My mind because so many people deal with hair and scalp issues. Alopecia or any other type of hair loss can be upsetting and stressful.

My thoughts were, "If I could build a product to free your mind, perhaps you'll find happiness again." I would like to prevent depression and anxiety for individuals struggling with hair loss by customizing wig units for them. By doing this, I'm freeing my mind with each unit given or sold, and that makes me happy. That is how I came up with my hair care/wig line, Free My Mind

Notes

Notes

Notes

Notes

Matthew 6:33

But seek ye first the kingdom of God, and his righteousness; and all these things shall be added unto you

It's Only One RACE! THE HUMAN RACE

Keep our Black, Hispanic, and all men in your prayers to live and not die! Jesus Christ died for all our sins, so why do some White American men and women think they are more Superior than BLACK American men or women?

Once the world accepts that there is only the human race, that is when WE as a people will win this racist disgrace.

Taking a Black man's life does not make you tough. It shows the world how weak you are and that you were always human, Punk!

Since many police officers are running around killing, maybe it's time Black Americans make them feel it.

So, Officer, how would it make you feel to watch your child get held down with a Black man's knee to his or her neck?

Will it make you lose all your respect for the black race?

SO WHY WAS THIS OK FOR YOU TO DO?

LEAVING A MOTHER TO RAISE ANOTHER DEAD MAN'S CHILD ON THE ACCOUNT OF POLICE ABUSE.

I HAVE HAD ENOUGH OF THIS SENSELESS, PAINFUL, WRONG KILLINGS!

I WILL KEEP SPEAKING OUT AND PRAYING TO GOD FOR US ALL TO RECEIVE HIS HEALING.

Notes

_____
_____
_____
_____
_____
_____
_____
_____
_____
_____
_____
_____
_____
_____
_____
_____
_____
_____
_____
_____
_____
_____
_____
_____
_____
_____
_____
_____
_____
_____
_____
_____

Notes

Notes

Notes

1st Corinthians 13:7-8

Rejoiceth not in iniquity, but rejoiceth in the truth;

Beareth all things, believing all things, endureth all things.

Note To Self

I have not done all that needs to be done in preparation for "DEDIVAS BBS, On The Run," and I am not giving up until I am doing GOD'S WILL. I AM A MULTIMILLIONAIRE in the making, and I am investing a ton, leaving a legacy for my six little ones. I had so many plans this year, Dudley EMS 2017, but I could not afford educational training with Nairobi. I was homeless, BROKE, and could NOT GO!

I had enough of what society says is poverty, from section 8, food stamps, and a broken community. I learned and accepted my mistakes. DeDIVAS BBS will be my escape. I said the year 2016 would be the last season of poverty. Just follow me and watch how God continues to set me free!

I encourage you all to educate and invest in yourselves and your children. Sometimes, investing can leave us clueless. No More! No More will I be a product of poverty! It's time I use my loss and invest in ME. I thank GOD for my struggles and tragedies; It made me stronger! Now I can see and believe, what's for me, IS FOR ME!

Notes

Notes

Notes

TOPIC: _____

Notes

1ˢᵗ Corinthians 13:13

And now abideth faith, hope, charity, these three; but the greatest of these is charity.

Journal To Self

My experience with Sports Clips

October 21st, I started a career at Sport Clips...

When I saw the hiring post on social media, I immediately responded to a lady named Morgan. I had no idea I was starting at a new store. I had just quit my job at Brightstar on October 12th, 2019. I thought to myself, "I am in debt with all my bills!"

- *Late fees from rent $455

- *Security deposit $750

- WE energies $280

- *Loan Max on My car, $1675 plus late fees

- Car registration $88

- Car Insurance $120

- Capital one $111

- Waterford ticket for car insurance $124

- IL Toll $1000

- Meadowood $960

- ATT Access $52

- Spectrum $216

DeDIVAS BBS - My brand has not grown or taken off. I have been trying and trying on my own since 2017. Today, I feel hopeless. I feel like my used-to-be family and friends do not support me. I feel like, "Dang Sophia, where did you go wrong?" You have a lot of talent; why are you struggling so bad? (Mentally, emotionally, and FINANCIALLY.)

At my psychiatrist session, I learned that I quit jobs because I am anxious, and if things become too much or hard for me, I just SHUT DOWN, QUIT, and want OUT. I will be going to outpatient services to help me cope with my Mental Health. (Learning about myself today really helped me a lot)

In the past years (since I was not successful at Glo' More or Heavenly Enhanced Suites), I learned that I needed clients in a suite and money to build my brand.

I needed marketing strategies and business direction. (I learned a lot through a book entitled When The Miracle Drops) After reading that book, I was ready; but I still lacked money!

I wanted to give up but had a goal in the back of my mind to start my business, April 2020. I needed the following in place:

- Website: iamsophiayamia.com
- Salon: Sophia Yamia's Artistry or Legacy
- Wig line; DDD-Legacy Bundles
- Complete my book coaching with Kenya Gray, M.D
- Destiny and Dejah's brand and Line

Which I will accomplish. I am very excited.

I also learned this year I am doing too many things. I had a lot going on this year. I guess because I was trying not to give up. Today, after learning more about anxiety, I see giving up is easy, and quitting jobs or not completing anything, can easily happen when stress/anxiety gets too high.

What are some things that have discouraged you from accomplishing your dreams?

Notes

Notes

TOPIC: _____

Notes

Notes

_____
_____
_____
_____
_____
_____
_____
_____
_____
_____
_____
_____
_____
_____
_____
_____
_____
_____
_____
_____
_____
_____
_____
_____
_____
_____
_____

Philippians 4:4-7

Rejoice in the Lord always: and again I say, Rejoice.

Let your moderation be known unto all men. The Lord is at hand.

Be careful for nothing; but in every thing by prayer and supplication with thanksgiving let your requests be made known unto God.

Sophia Yamia Degraffenreid

And the peace of God, which passeth all understanding, shall keep your hearts and minds through Christ Jesus.

I Still Have My Sanity, After Raising A Dead Man's Child

Man, how am I going to go to this man's funeral? I thought it was a dream, but it was My reality!

I was 16 years old and pregnant with my first child. As a matter of fact, it was my first son. I was still in high school and just getting home the night before, from spending the whole weekend with what we now call "My Bae." Yes, hunti, he was my bae, baby daddy, my EVERYTHING.

The problem was this was not just a bad dream. It was a Nightmare! A bad vision that I could not open my eyes and say, "Ok, It is just a dream. It is ok".

No, before I could open my eyes and wake up all the way, my phone was ringing, and it was my best friend. She was on the other end crying and trying so hard to be strong for me, trying to hold it together. She has always been so soft-spoken. She finally got it out, "Sophia, they killed Ken."

It's like, I already knew because I had just dreamt my first love, my Bae, my baby daddy, and my son's father had passed. "Funeral?" All I could do was jump up and down holding the telephone, crying, and screaming FROM MY BELLY AND THE BELLY OF MY UNBORN CHILD!

"WHYYYY??" My mom and dad came into the room, doing their best to comfort me. By this time, my best friend and her mother had arrived to comfort me and tell me what they knew. I had finally calmed myself down and got the ability to dial my Bae, Baby daddy, Boyfriend's phone number. The phone ranged; his father finally picked it up. I tried to sound normal, so I could get out my words of, "Hey Mr. Poppa, is Ken there?" Only to get the same response. My BFF Mo told me, "Budda Dead, Sophia!" They Killed Him"

I began the process all over—the scream of any woman who has lost their man, but forever.

All I could think of was, "DAMN! How will I go to this man's funeral?" I thought as I cried, paced, jumped, screamed, kicked, threw the phone, and hugged my family. "WHY DID THEY TAKE MY SON'S FATHER FROM ME? WHYYYYY! MY POOR BABY WON'T HAVE A DADDY!" All I wanted was to hear his voice again and for him to tell me he wasn't dead.

As the years went on, I learned to deal with my loss of one of the four most important men in my life. Ken Sr. My first child's father. Then five years later, my second child's father was forced to abandon me. My God, I thought my biological father abandoning me due to the jail system at age five would be the end, but it was actually the beginning of my life as an abandoned girl. My biological father was absent in my life—the one who builds the identity of his child. The only identity I had, was to engage in relationships with men who I knew would abandon me too.

You may be reading this book because you have experienced a form of abandonment in your life from a man you thought to be your everything;

Your father, the man who gives protection and identity to their child. But exactly how can a man, more so your father provide anything as such if he abandons you in any way? I know it hurts, but I am here to share my journey and next book, Raising A Dead Man's Child, Not Once but Twice, to help others address the hurt, pain, emptiness, and the whys of losing your father to jail and gun violence. I want to share how the father I know helped me cope with all the abandonment since I was five years old.

In loving memory of Kenneth D. Grays, and Donte L. Stamps

I pray this book loose healing unto all who reads...Coming soon

Notes

Notes

Notes

Notes

1st Thessalonians 5:17-18

Pray without ceasing.

In every thing give thanks: for
this is the will of God in Christ
Jesus concerning you

I DID IT, GURL!

Yes! On November 05, 2019, my 41st birthday, I checked into Rogers Behavior Health, Mental Health Recovery Program in Kenosha, Wisconsin. My psychiatrist referred me there, and praises be to God, I successfully completed treatment, and I celebrated my 42nd birthday looking fabulous and putting together my first journal!

U Did It Gurl is an empowerment anthem written by Sophia Degraffenreid, back in March 2013, after returning from Empire Beauty College.

"I wrote the song during my return to Dudley Beauty College, Chicago, IL.

As my ten-month Cosmetology Program leads into ten years, I did not let a time contract stop my journey. I had no quit in me. I was determined to obtain my cosmetology license and complete the program I started and was committed to. No matter how long it took me, no matter what adversities I faced, and no matter how many children I birthed during my ten-year season of hair school.

My first attempt at Cosmetology College began three months after I graduated from Rezin Orr Academy, high school, in 1998. I immediately enrolled and began what I thought was the beginning and end of my cosmetology journey at Truman College Chicago, Illinois, while living in a transitional teen mom shelter. Unfortunately, I had to drop that program because there was a shooting in my apartment building, and us teen moms had to vacate for a few weeks, causing me to be unstable again. I could no longer focus on my cosmetology program. Lord knows I wish I had because Truman College was offering an associate's degree while attending their cosmetology program.

I then moved out of Chicago to Zion, IL, where my mother, Sarai E. Fox, and Dad, Reginald Fox, raised my three sisters and I. I was awarded a Scholarship to attend DROS, Cosmetology School in North Chicago, Illinois, back in 2000, and would you believe ya gurl, Sophia Yamia, DROPPED that program? I wanted to work but could not work full time, raise two children, and go to vocational training in the evening. Boy, do I regret that decision. Had I known better, I would have done everything in my power to complete that local FREE program.

In the U Did It Gurl, Anthem, I am sharing my testimony of events that happened along my journey to the completion of Cosmetology school while sharing some of my childhood experiences with "bullying."

The day I sang the, U Did It Gurl Anthem on Facebook in February 2014, after passing my Illinois State board, other family and friends asked me to sing the U Did it Gurl, Anthem on Facebook. I was like, "I cannot keep singing this anthem for everyone." (lol), so I knew I had to get in the studio and drop my single. I am still working on the CD as I write this testimony and book.

After years of singing my song Acapulco for many accomplishments, I decided I wanted to put together a, U Did It Gurl hair show in September 2018, but that did not happen. As multiple women empowered me on putting together the hair show, I had a revelation that the U Did It Gurl, Anthem, was a movement. I began to use the hashtag #udiditgurl, leading to the, U Did It Gurl Empowerment brunch.

During my years of hoping to get a beat for my song, I began to type positive quotes on social media, learning it was a form of spoken word.

Today, as I write this book, I am now the songwriter, founder and now an author of The U

Did It Gurl, Empowerment Network, and U Did It Gurl, Empowerment Journal.

Praises be to God for allowing me to get through my adversities and continue my journey of success. I no longer see a young girl who used to help her mommy by braiding her hair and crying because her braids were so ugly. I see a young lady, braiding and styling hair during her high school years, who is now a Seasoned Woman. A business owner of a mobile salon, which all leads to my testimony, U Did It Girl Anthem, and U Did It Gul, Empowerment testimonial book.

Thank you all for taking the time to purchase my book and read it. Thank you all for allowing My book to EMPOWER AND INSPIRE YOU while on your journey to SUCCESS.

Blessings from,

~U DID IT GURL~

Notes

_____
_____
_____
_____
_____
_____
_____
_____
_____
_____
_____
_____
_____
_____
_____
_____
_____
_____
_____
_____
_____
_____
_____
_____
_____
_____
_____
_____
_____
_____
_____

Notes

_____
_____
_____
_____
_____
_____
_____
_____
_____
_____
_____
_____
_____
_____
_____
_____
_____
_____
_____
_____
_____
_____
_____
_____
_____
_____
_____
_____
_____
_____
_____
_____
_____
_____

Notes

Notes

Resource Page

Behavioral Health Services

▶ Lake County Health Department, Behavioral Health Services

3010 Grand Ave, Waukegan, IL, 60085

847-377-8000, Crisis, 1-847-377-8180

Website: www.lakecountyil.gov

▶Kenosha Community Health Center

Behavioral Health Services

4536 22nd Ave, Kenosha, WI, 53140

1-262-657-0044

Website: https://www.kenoshachc.org

►Amri Counseling Services

6321 23rd Ave, Kenosha, WI, 53143

414-455-3879

Website: amricouseling.com

►Family Psychiatric Care

1114 56th Street, Kenosha, WI, 53140

262- 725-4426

Website: https://fpckenosha.com

►Rogers Behavioral Health (Mental Health Recovery)

9916 75th Street, Suite 205

Kenosha, WI, 53142

1-262-942-4000

Website: rogersbh.org

▶ Worth Counseling

262-358-8008

Website: worthcounseling.com

▶*National Suicide Prevention Lifeline*

1-800-273- 8255

Cosmetology Education:

▶ Daisy's Resource and Developmental Center

1919 Dr. Daisy M. Brooks Drive

North Chicago, IL, 60064

Tel: 847-473-4898

Fax: 847-473-4908

Dr. Daisy M. Brooks -- CEO/President

Office 847-473-7081

Website: daisysrdc.com

▶ Dudley Beauty College

8501 S. Green Street, Chicago, IL, 60620

Made in the USA
Middletown, DE
15 April 2022